# SHARK

# SHARK

## Jeff Ross

*orca soundings*

ORCA BOOK PUBLISHERS

**Library and Archives Canada Cataloguing in Publication**

Ross, Jeff, 1973–, author
Shark / Jeff Ross.
(Orca soundings)

Issued in print and electronic formats.
ISBN 978-1-4598-1682-4 (softcover).—ISBN 978-1-4598-1683-1 (PDF).—
ISBN 978-1-4598-1684-8 (EPUB)

I. Title. II. Series: Orca soundings
PS8635.06928S53 2018      JC813'.6      C2017-904528-8
C2017-904529-6

First published in the United States, 2018
Library of Congress Control Number: 2017949692

**Summary:** In this high-interest novel for teen readers,
Mark "Shark" Hewitt is forced to play pool for profit.

MIX
Paper from
responsible sources
FSC® C016245
www.fsc.org

*Orca Book Publishers is dedicated to preserving the environment and has
printed this book on Forest Stewardship Council® certified paper.*

Orca Book Publishers gratefully acknowledges the support for its
publishing programs provided by the following agencies: the Government
of Canada through the Canada Book Fund and the Canada Council
for the Arts, and the Province of British Columbia through
the BC Arts Council and the Book Publishing Tax Credit.

Edited by Tanya Trafford
Cover image by iStock.com and Shutterstock.com

ORCA BOOK PUBLISHERS
www.orcabook.com

Printed and bound in Canada.

21  20  19  18  •  4  3  2  1

*For Mark Molnar*

# Chapter One

The place was called Minnesota's, a cavernous room beneath a strip mall full of respectable suburban shops. The sign outside continued to inform that Halloween was upon us, even though it was the end of February. Inside, rows of pool tables ran the length of the room, buffered from the walls by pinball and vintage video-game machines.

The soundtrack was classic rock, balls clacking off one another and bursts of excited cheering. The fragrance: spilled beer and cigarettes smoked a decade before.

It felt, in every way possible, like home.

I found Minnesota's when my mom, sister and I moved here a month ago. The regulars were cool and always looking for a game. The owner was happy to give the odd free ginger ale when I'd been there a while. But best of all, there was absolutely no betting permitted.

I had sunk the three and the five when I noticed this guy watching me from a couple of tables away. He was tall, thickset, with an unruly mess of hair on his head and an equally untamed beard on his face. I'd never seen him before. His clothes screamed biker—the leather vest over printed T, extremely blue jeans cinched up with an extra-large buckled, studded belt.

"Am I going to get to play this game?"

I looked across the table at Hippy. He was tall and thin, dropped into a vintage Pearl Jam shirt and cargo pants. Sandals over thick socks in the dead of winter. He was the day manager but always found time for a couple of games.

The one and the four were left on the table for me. Plus the eight ball, of course. The one was an easy shot. The four, way more difficult. I was challenging myself to not take the easy shot. I lined up the four, and Hippy clicked his tongue. He did this every time he saw an easier shot available. I figured he'd catch on to what I was doing someday.

The four bounced off the edge of the corner pocket and sat there spinning.

"Yes," Hippy said. "I shall now destroy you." He pulled his long hair from his face and leaned over the table.

I sat on a high stool and, pretending to watch Hippy take his shot, glanced over at the biker guy. He'd gone back to playing alone on one of the large snooker tables.

"Come on fifteen, don't be cruel," Hippy said, leaning low to the table. It looked like he was attempting to send the ball into a pocket by sheer force of will. But the fifteen just sat there, right on the cusp of the pocket. Hippy stood to his full height and rubbed his stubbled chin. "All right, Shark, finish me off."

I leaned over the table and focused on the four, which was now an easy shot. Or, at least, no more difficult than the one.

"Shark?" I looked up to find the biker guy at the end of the table, looking right at me.

"It's just a nickname," I said. I didn't want to get into the whole thing. My name's Mark, but when I was younger my little sister put an S on the front of a lot of her words, and so to my family I became Shark. I'd told Hippy this story one day and instantly regretted it.

"Looks earned to me," biker guy said.

"Hippy," a waitress called from behind the bar. "That thing's backed up again."

Hippy shook his head and set his cue into the wall rack. "You play him, War," Hippy said. "I have to take care of this."

"War?" I said.

"Nickname," the biker guy said. "Name's Warren." He stepped forward and extended a hand. I shook it, then got low to the table again to finish the game Hippy and I had been playing.

I wasn't sure I wanted to play War that evening. The whole feeling of the

5

pool hall changed for me the instant Hippy walked away. Everything got heavy, if that's a way to describe it. I don't know—I've never been that good with words.

"Good to meet you," I said.

I finished the game easily. The one and four found pockets, and after bouncing the cue off two bumpers, I sank the eight.

War began racking the balls into the triangle. "Where'd you learn to play?" he asked.

I sat on the high stool again and took a sip from the ginger ale I'd been working on.

"My dad," I said, leaving it at that.

"Basement table?" He wiggled the balls in the triangle until they were tight, then slowly lifted the frame off the table.

"Mostly pool halls," I said.

War picked up his cue. "So," he said, leaning down to set his aim on the cue ball. "Where's dad now?"

"Not around," I said. War was drawing his cue back and forth. It was my table though. Whenever you win a game, you own the table. If someone wants to play you, they have to let you break. It's etiquette, but the kind of etiquette that is pretty much a rule.

He hammered the cue ball into the triangle of balls. I watched as they spread out across the table. The fifteen and twelve dropped, but the cue ball settled in right behind the three. In eight-ball, you're either low ball or high. That means you either have to get balls one through seven in, or the nine through fifteen. And then, of course, to finish it off, the eight. When you break and sink a couple of balls, you have the advantage of taking a follow-up shot to decide whether it's the low or high end you need to play.

"That's too bad," War said. I thought he was talking about where the cue ball was sitting, but then he continued. "My dad ditched when I was twelve." I let him take his shot. He decided against the four, which was perfectly lined up, hoping, it seemed, to get the eleven in and play the high balls. Instead, he tapped the eleven into the perfect position for me to sink it.

"You're low ball," I said. I didn't want to talk about my dad. I went to pool halls to feel close to him. Playing pool was the one thing we had done together that hadn't ended badly. It was the time I had felt most connected to my dad. But that was all in the past, and if I've learned anything, it's that it's best to leave it there.

The remaining high balls were in perfect positions for me to run the table. Which was exactly what I did. I didn't feel the need to hold back.

"Nicely done," War said when I'd finished. "Another?"

I checked my phone. Almost seven already. "Not tonight," I said. "I have to go." I shrugged into my jacket.

War came over to shake my hand. "That was a hell of a game," he said.

"Thanks." I shook his hand. "Maybe play again sometime?"

He let go of my hand. "Sounds good," he said with a smile. "I'll be here practicing."

His smile felt genuine. It seemed kind. It lit up his face in a way that reminded me of the only nice teacher I'd ever had.

I got home right as Mom was heading out the door.

"Mark," she said. "Why are you so late?"

"Sorry," I said. I didn't need to tell her I'd been at a pool hall. She already knew.

"Have you eaten?" Her hair was a bird's nest. Whenever she got anxious, she ran her hand through it, and I knew, standing there on the porch, that my being late had made her worry.

"Not yet."

"There's some casserole in the kitchen. Wendy is doing her homework. Can you help her with it?"

"Absolutely," I said.

My little sister is twelve. She is old enough to stay home alone but has always been easily freaked out. Mom doesn't like leaving her alone for very long.

I went inside, dished out a bowl of casserole and put it in the microwave. I sat down at the table. Wendy had a sheet of math problems in front of her. They'd been working on geometry in class, and she was not liking it much. Personally, I love geometry. Everything I did growing up had to do with angles.

I'd been a goalie for a while. A good one too. Every year since Atom, I'd been on the AAA competitive team. I think it was easier for me than for some other kids because it was all about the angles.

And I dreamed in angles.

"These are great," I said.

"Math homework is great, Mark?" Wendy said. Her knees were bundled up beneath her. She's small for her age, so sitting like that was the only way she could see the work on the table. My mom's pretty small too, and they share the crazy-curly hair.

"It is when it's geometry."

She sighed her most expressive sigh. She is artsy. Math feels like an unnecessary punishment to her, whereas for me it was the only real reason I went to school.

I pointed at one of the diagrams. "This one is beautiful. Poetry in motion."

"Wrong," she said.

"For me," I said, standing as the microwave binged, "there is nothing more beautiful than what you see before you this moment."

Wendy sighed again and dropped her head on the table.

"Then you do it," she said, pushing the paper away.

"No way," I said, sitting back down with my steaming bowl. "You need to find the beauty yourself."

Wendy banged her head against my shoulder. "There is no beauty here," she said. "It's just stupid lines and numbers."

I closed my eyes and inhaled. "Lines and numbers, Wendy, is what the world is made of." I opened my eyes to find my sister making a face with puffed-out cheeks and huge round eyes. I grabbed her pencil, pretended to pop her cheeks and said, "Here, let me show you."

# Chapter Two

I'd started playing hockey around the same time my dad introduced me to pool. First I was a forward, and then, after trying it just one time, I found that I loved being a goalie. Looking back, I now understand it was all about the angles. Staying square to the shooter so he couldn't see the net. Shifting to cut off a backdoor pass. Watching only the puck, never the player. Seeing the angle.

My dad got really into watching me play. The problem was, he could be a bit of a hothead. He'd yell at the refs, who would ignore him. He'd yell at the coaches on both benches. They did their best to ignore him as well. He'd even yell at some of the kids on the ice when he got really fired up.

Then one game, when I was twelve, he went a step too far.

There was this one kid on this one team who everyone knew about. He seemed to believe he was in an NHL arena and two feet taller than he was in reality. He'd line kids up for hits when any kind of contact meant an immediate penalty. He always kept an eye on the refs to see where they were looking before he committed his most brazen fouls. At some point he must have decided that the best strategy was to mess with the opposing goalie.

Every game, this kid ran the goalie. At first, he'd stop at the top of the crease and spray the goalie a few times. But soon he elevated this to going hard into the net and "accidentally on purpose" falling and taking out the goalie at the knees. It had happened to me twice in that season, so I was ready for him that day.

He kept looking my way, but for the first period he was never on the ice when the puck came down to our end. We were owning his team after the first period, 3–0, and I could tell he was frustrated. He took the face-off on the first puck drop of the second period and banged the puck ahead, spinning our center around as he tore past. I banged my catcher and got ready for him. He gained a ton of speed and then fell about ten feet out, blades up in front of him and aimed right at me. I didn't even bother with the puck. If it happened to trickle in after he'd rammed me, it would be called a no goal because of goaltender interference. So for once I took my eyes off the puck and instead waited for him to slide in. When he did, I jumped up and came down hard with my pads on his stupid head.

He made the most amazing whimpering sound I'd ever heard. Soon enough, though, he was flailing around and punching and kicking. He knocked both our helmets off, and a second later I was punching him in the head. I'm not a violent person, but with this happening every game and no one seeming to want to stop it, I had to take matters into my own hands.

We both received penalties on the play. I stayed on the ice, because another player has to serve any penalties a goalie gets, while the kid was taken to the dressing room. I was shaking and felt sick after it. My dad yelling at the kid's father didn't make things any better. We won that game, although the handshake line at the end was intense.

Dad lost his mind over the remainder of the game. When I found him in the lobby he was seething and banging his fists on things.

Settle down, Morgan, one of the other dads said. Everyone's all right.

That kid has to be stopped, my dad replied. Then he grabbed my stick and banged through the doors into the frigid parking lot.

He was protecting me—I can see that now. But for anyone else, it must have looked like one more Morgan Hewitt moment of uncontrollable rage. Something he needed to reel in. But from his perspective, my dad was just worried I was going to get hurt. This was the only way he could protect me.

Out in the parking lot, he spotted the kid's dad. I watched as he grabbed the man by the shoulder and spun him around. He said, Your asshole kid is going to get someone seriously injured one of these days. I'm going to do everything I can to get him kicked out of the league.

The kid's dad got this smug look on his face and laughed. You're just upset because your kid's a sieve, he said.

Which totally wasn't true. We'd won that game four to one, and the other team's one goal was a deflection off my defender's skate. But just hearing him say it made me angry as well.

Hard to make stops when you have some fat moron sitting on your head, Dad said. He was shaking my goalie stick at the man. That action would come back to haunt him.

Your kid is afraid to play hard. This is hockey, not T-ball, the man said.

Your kid's a thug, Dad said. His only skill is falling down.

The kid's dad threw the first punch. My dad managed to dodge it and immediately toss his own haymaker. If you've never seen your dad in a fight in a freezing-cold parking lot in the dim light of evening, I envy you. It's horrible. They both looked uncoordinated. They both were red in the face with rage. They both were behaving like complete idiots.

I remember standing there with all my gear, my pads hanging over my shoulder, and all I wanted to do was get in the car and go home. I'd seen my dad angry and yelling at people before, but he'd never been in a fight.

He threw my stick to the ground, and I walked over to get it.

What ended up taking out the other kid's dad had pretty much nothing to do with my dad. The kid's dad threw a punch, missed, spun around in a half circle and fell to the ground. People who had gathered to watch this spectacle laughed. It looked ridiculous. The thing was, he didn't get up.

And then we saw the blood.

His son was down beside him, shaking his shoulder, yelling in his ear, looking up at everyone as though someone could help. But no one could help. His dad died in that frosty parking lot. Though it wasn't a punch or shove from my dad that caused the final injury, Dad ended up going to jail for manslaughter. They had been in a fight. If the fight had never happened, the kid's dad would still be alive. My dad had grabbed the man's shoulder and spun him around first. He'd shaken my goalie stick at the guy in a threatening manner. Everyone testified to that.

Even I had to testify to that.

Thinking back, as I often do, my most vivid memory is of the blood spreading onto the parking block. Yet at the time,

I remember, all I could see were the angles—his body, the parking block perpendicular to his outstretched arm, and the long line of blood creating an almost perfect triangle.

## Chapter Three

I walked Wendy home after school the next day. Mom was still at work, but Wendy was okay being by herself as long as it was light out.

The pool hall was a bus ride away, which sucked. We only had one car, so although I had my driver's license, there was never a vehicle for me to use. I have often thought that if I wasn't killing time in pool halls, I could have a job and make some real money. Maybe get a real car, a girlfriend—a life.

A tournament was beginning when I entered Minnesota's. Ten dollars a player, winner takes all. There were a dozen of us there, so you could walk away with over a hundred bucks. The tournament was immediate elimination. Game to game, table to table, lose and you were done.

I had ten dollars, so I threw it in, figuring that if I ended up winning, it would be a good day. I could use it to take Mom and Wendy out for dinner.

"Shit, are you in this, Shark?"

I turned to find War leaning against the table. "I guess I am now."

"I'm going to have to step up my game." He put his hand out, and I shook it. "Good luck," he said.

"Same to you."

For the first game I was paired up with this older man whose belly was so big he had to shift sideways whenever he sidled up to the table. He wasn't much competition, and I think he knew it, but he was clearly enjoying the atmosphere. I made fairly short work of him, and he gave me a good, firm handshake when it was over. Some of the other tables took longer, so I sat and watched, seeing what kind of game everyone played.

My next opponent was a lady with kinky brown hair, glasses, a pool glove and a pink cue. I'd seen her around before. She played a nice steady game, always making clean shots and bringing the cue ball into place for her next shot.

We flipped for break, and I won.

"Uh-oh," she said.

"What?" I replied.

"I've seen you play, kid. And I have a feeling this tournament is about to be over for me."

I got a beautiful break. All the low balls sat there, waiting to find their home in the pockets. I worked the table, chalking between shots. Two balls in one pocket, brought the cue ball back to get two more quickly. Chalk, chalk. I went into a different head space, and soon all I had left was the eight, which was sitting right in the middle of the table, a wall of high balls surrounding it. I hammered the cue ball to get the eight ball moving, then sat down.

"Thank you very much for letting me play," the woman said. I'd heard someone call her Tracy before.

"I didn't have many options, Tracy," I said, immediately realizing I sounded dickish. I attempted to recover. "I've seen you play, and now I'm the one whose tournament might be over."

"Sweet of you to say," she replied. She sank four in a row before the cue ball drifted into a side pocket after coming off a bumper strangely. I brought it out of the pocket and quickly sank the eight.

"And…I'm done," Tracy said.

"Good game," I said.

"That was about as good as I get." She smiled, and I felt bad about being a jerk before. I do that sometimes. I say things without thinking how they're going to sound.

"Thank you for the game," I said.

"You're welcome." She leaned into me. "I hope you win it all. You deserve it." I felt a bit uncomfortable. To be honest, I don't enjoy it when pool turns into a competition. I am always competing with myself. Pushing to get better. So it was difficult to see someone "lose" because I won.

And just like that, we were down to three. Myself, this business-looking dude, and War. We flipped coins to see who would play the next game and who would wait for the final. I won, which meant I had to sit and wait for War and the other dude to play. This made me even more anxious, as it was six thirty and I was getting tight for time. I went to the far wall and called my mom. I told her I might be a little late because of the bus. I hated lying to her, but honestly, the bus did only run every half hour, and I'd likely just missed one.

"That's all right," she said. "Wendy has finished her homework and is watching TV. You have your key?"

"Yes."

"I'll lock up, but don't be too late."

"Okay." I returned to the table. War and the other guy were standing there looking at the collection of balls. Talking.

Hippy came across to watch the game. He leaned on the high table beside me. "These guys go on forever," he said.

"Really?"

"Epic matches."

I watched with increasing frustration. Both War and the other guy seemed to need to vocalize every one of their thoughts. It was excruciating.

It was a quarter after seven before I got to the table.

"We meet again," War said. He put his hand out, and I shook it before taking up the triangle and racking the balls. "I get the break."

"If that's how it works," I replied.

"It isn't in the rules that way, man," Hippy said. The hall was mostly empty, so he'd stayed around to watch the whole tournament unfold, I guess. War didn't respond. Hippy shrugged and as he sat down again, said, "As if anyone reads those."

"I'm fine with that," I said, stepping away from the table. Everyone who had been in the tournament gathered around.

"I get this feeling I'd better clear the table right off the break or it'll be curtains," War said. A couple of people laughed.

The first guy I'd played said, "That's what happened to me." Even though it wasn't true.

War's break was pretty good but left a cluster of the low balls around the eight, tight against a pocket. There would have to be some delicate maneuvers to get those somewhere you could work with them.

War scratched on his next shot, leaving the table open.

"Shit," he said. He chalked his cue and shook his head. "You've got me nervous, kid."

I sank half of the high balls, but then I bumped the eleven a little too lightly. It sat hovering on the edge of a pocket.

"All right then," War said. "Back in the game." He walked the table, looking for an angle on the three low balls still clustered around the eight. "Think I can squeak that four past the eight?"

"I don't know," I said. "I don't really give advice."

"I'm not looking for advice. I'm just wondering what you think. You have thoughts on this, right?"

"I don't know what you're capable of," I said.

His blue eyes bore into me with an unnerving intensity. "Hmm," he said, nodding at me, then at the table.

He took forever to figure out his shot. Lining it up one way and then another. If I'd actually felt like giving him advice, I would have suggested he run the cue ball in and snooker me on the next shot. It was a dick move for sure, but there was no way I could tap the eleven in from that angle. Instead he lined up one of his balls, drilled it in with a little too much force and sank both it and the eight ball.

"Son of a bitch," he said. "There you go. Worst way to win."

"It is," I said.

War banged his cue against the back of a chair, then shook my hand. "I'll get you one of these days."

"I'm sure you will," I said.

Hippy came over to the table. "There you go, Mark," he said, handing me the money.

I quickly jammed the bills into my pocket and then looked at my phone. Quarter after eight. "Shit, I have to go." I pulled my jacket on and ran up the stairs to street level just in time to see the bus I needed fly past. I didn't want to wait half an hour for the next one. I considered taking a taxi, but even with what I had just won, I hated to spend that kind of money just to get from one place to another. I got my phone out and stared at it. I didn't want to call Mom. I could call Wendy and tell her I'd be late. But that would freak her out after what had happened with Dad. We had learned the hard way that life could suddenly take a turn no one was expecting. And we were coping in different ways. I played pool. Wendy made schedules and needed to know where Mom and I were at all times.

I had to get home but could see no way to do it. I stood there staring at my phone, wondering what the hell I was going to do.

# Chapter Four

"You all right, Shark?" I turned around to find War coming up behind me.

"I missed my bus," I said. He was stopped beside a big blue pickup truck.

"Hop in," he said. "I'll give you a ride."

"That's okay." I was shivering inside my jacket.

He looked up the empty street. "The next bus won't be for ages, right?"

"Half an hour," I said, looking at the truck the way frozen travelers look at smoke coming from a cabin's chimney.

"What part of town are you in?"

I told him.

"That's on my way. Come on, hop in." I thought about this for a moment and then darted across the lot and climbed in. The cab was not as warm as I'd hoped, although once we hit the road, the heavy heat from the vents quickly filled the space.

"Where'd you come from?" War asked as he lit a cigarette.

"Rez Falls," I replied.

"Over by Morrisberg?"

"Yup."

"Nice area. What did you come here for?" The truck smelled of cigarettes and minty gum. There were two Big Gulp cups from 7-Eleven in the holders between the seats. Both of the lids were stained, leaving me to believe they'd been there a while.

"My mom got a job as a pharmacist's assistant."

"Which pharmacy?" War asked.

"Ray's on Main."

"Ray's cool," War said. He shifted in his seat. "What about your dad?"

I bristled at the question. We'd started at a new school in September. Wendy had made friends, but I'd yet to settle into a crowd. It's a lot easier when you're in middle school. I'd never really hidden what had happened with my dad. There wasn't a reason to. But every time I told the story, I felt something right in the middle of my chest. It didn't exactly hurt, but it felt wrong.

"He's in jail," I said. Then I gave War the short version of the story.

"That is for shit," he said. "Things happen." He shrugged as if to say it was no big deal. Not the fact that Dad was in jail, but that what I'd just told him didn't affect the way he saw me.

What had happened to my dad had taught me one thing—to keep my anger in check. You have to keep all your emotions in check. You can't get too high or too low. I don't know if my dad was able to control his anger at all. I'm not sure he ever tried.

We pulled up outside the house. All the lights were on. This was how Wendy compensated for being alone. She kept the place looking like a dozen people were inside. She'd be watching TV, the volume low so she could hear if anyone, or anything, crept through the door.

"Thanks for the ride," I said. "You really saved me there."

"No problem, Shark. No problem. Hey, listen, I need to take a leak. Mind if I come in?" He looked over me at the house. I didn't like the idea, but

Warren seemed okay. Nothing there to make me think he'd be a problem. Somehow I'd decided he was one of those tough-looking guys who is actually a teddy bear.

"Sure, okay," I said. "My sister's here."

"You have a sister?" he said, but not in a creepy way. "Is she older or younger?"

"Twelve."

"All right, I'll be quiet. In and out," he said, opening the truck door.

"Hey, Wendy," I yelled when I stepped in.

"You're back!" she said, calling from the living room. "Come see this angel I drew."

"Listen, I have a friend here. He's going to use the bathroom."

"Oh. Okay," she replied, her voice suddenly uncertain. She didn't like me bringing people into the house. Especially men.

"Bathroom's down there," I said to War. He stomped through the house, his cowboy boots clicking on our hardwood. I stuck my head into the living room and found Wendy on the floor in front of the coffee table, drawing something, the TV on low.

"Good day?" I asked.

"Yeah," she said. "We got double art."

"How'd that happen?"

"The gym teacher was sick."

"This must have been the best day of your year." She hates gym.

"It was," she said. Something on the TV show grabbed her attention. I looked back and there was War, standing outside the bathroom.

"Thanks for that, man," he said. He walked into the kitchen and looked around. "Nice place."

"We're renting," I said.

"I know these homes. My old man used to be in the trades. He did a lot of the plumbing on these places when they were built." War kept moving around the kitchen. "He did a lot of the tiles as well. He might have laid this floor."

"That's cool," I said. War smiled at the room as if he was proud of it. As if he was standing in the middle of something his father had created.

He grabbed a photo of Mom, Wendy and me off the fridge. "Good-looking family," he said.

"Thanks," I replied.

"I think I've seen your mom before. At Ray's, right?"

"Yeah," I said. He made another circle of the kitchen and then headed into the living room. We don't have much stuff, and what we do have is kind of regular. Nothing fancy.

"Hi there," he said to Wendy. My sister gave him a half smile and wave.

He glanced at the TV, then returned to the kitchen.

"All right, Shark," he said, putting his hand on my shoulder. "Thanks for the game tonight. I'll get you next time." He squeezed in a way that made me squirm out of his grasp.

"I'm sure you will." I walked him to the hallway, thanked him for the ride and shut the door behind him. For some reason, I watched him through one of the little squares of glass in the door, standing off to one side in case he looked back. He went straight to his truck, but then, just before he got in, he stopped for a second, stared at the house and gave it a little nod. I figured he was feeling family pride. And that was cool. His dad had helped put this place together, and now my family lived in it. That would have been a great feeling.

Too bad I was wrong.

## Chapter Five

I didn't tell Mom anything about War having been in the house. I didn't think she'd like it. I thought she was still a little afraid of men too. It didn't seem like anything the next day anyway. Just someone who'd given me a lift home. He'd needed to use the bathroom, and I let him.

No harm.

All day I thought about playing pool. It was my standard daydream. When I closed my eyes I could see balls spinning, dropping, sliding up the bumpers.

On the way home from school I stopped by to pick up Wendy. She was excited. She told me all about her art class and how her English teacher was going to get them to write short stories. She told me about this really creepy story they had read, called "The Lottery." It was all about how the people in this town thought they were entering a lottery where they'd win some big prize, but in the end it was all about choosing someone to be sacrificed. Or maybe the townspeople knew what was happening but the reader doesn't. I couldn't totally tell.

"That sounds really weird," I said.

"You've never read it?" Wendy said. "It's the best. You don't know what is going to happen, and then when it does, it is crazy. You have to read it."

"But you already told me what happens."

"I guess, but it's still worth it."

We came in the back way that day, cutting through the neighbor's yard. Wendy ran inside yelling, "Mom! Have you ever read 'The Lottery'?"

I stopped. Something about the house, I couldn't say what, felt different.

"Hey, hon," I heard Mom say. "Your brother with you?"

"Yeah, I'm here," I said, shutting the door behind me.

"Oh, good. Mark, your friend is here."

Friend? I didn't have any friends. No one at the school anyway. I stepped into the living room, and there was War sitting on the couch.

"Mark," Mom said, "Warren said you had plans to meet up?"

War looked different. He'd washed up, cut his hair and trimmed his beard. And he'd swapped out his leather vest and jeans for a respectable pair of gray trousers and a bright-blue sweater. He looked like his more successful twin brother.

"Hey, Shark, how are you?"

"Good," I said. "I don't remember us making plans."

"I was telling your mom about that tournament last night. I haven't been able to get it out of my head. We need a rematch, son." Something made me shiver, and, again, I didn't know exactly what. Something just seemed different. Or maybe it was just that I was waiting for Mom to flip out on me because I hadn't told her about the tournament.

"Sure," I said. "We can do that sometime."

Mom said, "I don't mind you taking off with Warren now if you want. As long as you're back by seven."

"Not tonight," I said. "I have homework to do."

"Come on, Shark. Best of three," War said. He smiled.

I could feel my fingers twitching. I'd wanted to play pool all day, and here was my opportunity.

"Okay, sure, why not?" I said. "But only three games."

Warren smiled and clapped his hands. "I'm winning two of them," he promised.

"Warren was telling me about the charity he works with. What was it called?"

"Kids with Kicks," Warren said. "We get kids playing soccer in the summer and then open up a community center in the winter for them."

"That sounds great," Mom said. "Doesn't that sound great, Mark?" Wendy had disappeared to her room.

"Sounds great, yeah." I guess I could have sounded a bit more enthusiastic, but I hate soccer.

"Let's do this," War said, standing. He gave my mother a little bow. "Thank you for your hospitality."

"My pleasure," Mom said.

My mom was smiling at him. A genuine smile. Something I had not seen in a long while.

"Later," I said, before closing the door.

"Have fun!" she called back.

Minnesota's was filled with the sound of clacking balls and laughter. Just coming down the stairs sent me back to the days with my dad.

"Eight- or nine-ball?" War asked.

"Nine," I said. Dad and I had always started with a game of nine-ball. War racked them and stepped away from the table. I managed to clear the table from the break. That happens in nine-ball way more than in eight. It was a great way to start. One ball after the other until they were all gone.

"Well," War said, laughing. He nodded his head and started racking again. "You're a hell of a player."

"Those ones lined up for me," I said. "I got lucky."

"I don't think you get lucky," War said, lifting the triangle. "I think you see the table like very few people do."

I didn't respond. I did, however, back away from the table. "You can break," I said.

"Not how I play," War said. "You won, you break." This was different than the night before at the tournament. Then, War wasn't going to give up the table even if he had to cheat to break. But with nothing riding on the game, I figured he didn't care. I was totally in the mood for playing that night, so it made no difference to me. I wanted to clear the table again and again. That's the thing about pool—you might be up against someone else, but in the end you're really only playing yourself. You play the table and very rarely worry about what your opponent is going to do.

The balls lined up perfectly. Half of them sat right beside pockets. The rest were within, at most, a single bounce off a bumper. I moved around the table, chalking, aiming and sinking balls until the table was, yet again, empty.

"Well, I guess you've won the best of three," War said, racking. "Want another?"

"Absolutely," I said. I felt like I could play all night

"Am I going to get to play this time?"

"Maybe," I said. "Maybe not." We both laughed, though I could tell War was getting irritated. When he pulled the triangle up, he shifted it slightly, edging a couple of balls away from the pack. This might not seem like anything, but when the balls aren't tight to one another, it really affects the break. And, sure enough, my break went wild. The balls on the outside spun off in all directions, but a clump of balls remained as though not struck at all.

The seven dropped, and then I was able to sink the one and two before missing on the three. War stood up and leaned over the table.

"So you never play for money," he said.

"The odd tournament," I said. "Like last night. Those are okay. It's all out in the open there."

"What do you mean?" War asked, firing the four and then five in opposite corners. He played a very slow and deliberate game. Always lining his shots up with a practiced care.

"You put in ten dollars or whatever and then get to play. No one is getting cheated," I said.

"But you wouldn't play for money in a pool hall?"

"It feels too personal," I said. "In a tournament, you take someone out and then have the next opponent to deal with. When you get to the end, it's everyone's money you're playing for. It's different."

"You could clean up," War said.

I shrugged and leaned back over the table. I managed to get to the nine and somehow left it sitting in the middle of the table. At first I couldn't say why this happened, but afterward, once we were back outside and sitting in War's truck, I realized it was because War had been watching me. Not watching the game, but staring at me. I'd turned around a couple of times, and he'd been looking right at me.

He did the same thing as we pulled up to a red light.

"So you have absolutely no interest at all in playing for money," he said. At the time I had no idea why he kept asking.

"No," I said. "I know I should. Or at least get into a league or something. But it's not me."

"Not even if I told you you could make a lot of money? That I could help make that happen?"

"No," I said. "Sorry."

When we pulled up outside my house, War put the truck into Park in the same thoughtful way he played pool. Not slamming the gearshift but moving it slowly into place. He drove the same way. There were no quick jumps off red lights or tight, tire-squawking turns. He did everything in a perfectly methodical way.

"Thanks," I said. He gave me a half smile, his blue eyes boring holes in me again. I jumped out of the truck and turned back to close the door, but he'd already leaned across the seat and taken hold of the handle.

"Sure, Shark," he said. "No problem. See you tomorrow."

## Chapter Six

And just like that, War was around all the time. The next morning he stopped by to fix a broken tile he'd seen. He told my mother the story about his father being the one who'd put it in and that he felt responsible for fixing it. She happened to mention a dripping faucet in the basement that the landlord had promised to come by and fix but never had. It wasn't her problem if he didn't care, but she hated being wasteful. War returned the next day to fix that. He was normally gone by the time Wendy and I got home from school, but his odor, a mix of sweat and cologne, lingered.

It was a few days before I saw him at the pool hall again.

I'd been playing Hippy for almost two hours. He was always up for a fun game and was good enough to give me a challenge. Then War walked in, looking clean-cut although upholding his biker image with a beat-up leather jacket. When he unzipped it, I could see the bright-blue sweater glowing underneath.

"Mark," he said. "How are you?"

"Great," I replied. I was in the middle of a game.

He pointed to the far end of the room. "League night," he said, giving me a pat on the back. "Talk later, okay?"

I noticed he smiled at Hippy before walking away.

"I don't know about that guy," Hippy said. "You hang out with him a lot?"

I finished my shot and leaned against the table. "He's kind of around now," I said.

"What do you think of him?" he asked.

I considered this for a moment and had to admit, "I don't know. I guess he's all right?"

"I don't know anything about him. But he has this vibe, man. Not a good one."

I played Hippy for a while longer, until it started to feel late. I decided to leave with plenty of time to make my bus this time rather than play one last game and risk missing it. The league tournament was still going on when I left. I was standing at the bus stop when War came banging out the front door of the hall.

"Shark! One minute, son." He lit a cigarette as he crossed the parking lot. Was the old, scruffy War the real deal, or was it this new clean-cut Warren? Either way, I was getting an uneasy feeling as he came toward me.

"Let me give you a lift home," he said.

"I'm good," I said, holding up my bus pass.

"Nah, come on. I'm going to pick your mom up from Ray's as well."

"What?"

"She called earlier. Her car broke down, and she's stuck. I told her I'd give her a lift home and get someone to come tow her car to my buddy's garage."

Huh. The pharmacy was only a few blocks away, so I didn't get the chance to ask how it came about that my mom had called him. But then, what would

I have said? What are your intentions with my mother? Why are you suddenly a part of my life? That sounded rude, and at the time, War seemed nice enough. I mean, Warren of the blue sweater and slick hair. He peeled the leather jacket off when he got into the truck and tossed it to the backseat. Then he checked his hair in the mirror and dropped the truck into gear.

I slipped into the backseat of the cab when my mom got in. She and War chatted about all kinds of things I wouldn't have suspected they would talk about. Even the possibility that Mom might go visit Dad. She hadn't seen him in ages. For some reason, though, she was suddenly thinking of going.

When we got home, War got a call from his buddy to let him know that everything was okay with the car. It wasn't anything serious. He'd fix it that night, off the books, for the cost of parts and enough for him to get some dinner and a case of beer.

"Thank you so much, Warren," Mom said.

"No problem. Glenn likes to tinker. He could mess around with those things all day. You might want to think about looking for a new car sometime soon though."

"Maybe," Mom said.

"You're working awful hard. You should be able to afford something, right?"

"Legal fees," Mom said. "It takes a lot." Warren sat there watching her until she clapped her hands. "Okay, dinner!"

"Yes," War said. "A home-cooked meal." I hadn't known that War was staying for dinner. Mom had one special meal she loved to make. She knew it would always be perfect. It was this kind of baked chicken thing with a sauce her grandmother had come up with.

A salad on the side and a baked potato with garlic butter and chives. War enjoyed it as if he hadn't eaten a real meal in years. He was *mmmm*ing and licking his lips and looking around as if there might be seconds. Nothing made my mom happier than someone enjoying her cooking. It wasn't necessarily something she took pride in, but she did love when people enjoyed it.

"The kids have homework to do, I imagine," War said once dinner was finished. He'd stacked the dishes in the sink against mom's protests. "Don't want to get in the way here."

"Oh, you can stay a little longer," Mom said.

"No, I've always believed it's best to leave when you're still welcome." He looked over at me and smiled. "Say, Shark, I have that book I was telling you about out in the truck. I forgot to give it to you earlier."

"What book?" I said. I was pretty sure he hadn't mentioned a book.

"Come on out. I'll show you." He bowed again to Mom and, holding both her hands in his, said, "Until next time."

It was cold outside, with a sharp, biting wind washing up the street. War opened the door of his truck as if he was going to grab something. Then he turned to me. There was a look on his face I'd never seen before.

"And just like that," he said, snapping his fingers, "I'm in your life." He narrowed his eyes at me.

"What?" I said. I was still trying to figure out where the book was that he wanted to give me.

"Your mom loves me. She's eating it up."

"What are you talking about?" A cold shiver shot through my body.

"I'm a nice guy, Shark. The kind of man you'd want your kid to hang

around with while his dad's locked up."
He stared at the house again.

"What are you talking about, War?"

"I'm here now," he said, still staring
at the house. "The question is, do I want
to stay?"

"Stay?" I said. I felt as if I couldn't
move. Like my feet had taken root in the
ground.

"I have a plan A and a plan B. Plan
A, I get into your life and then when I
ask you to help me make some money,
you can't say no. You wouldn't want
to disappoint your mom, after all. Plan
B, I get into your life and I stay." I was
starting to understand what he was
talking about. I understood what that
look had been on his face.

It was the look of an initial victory in
a long battle.

"If you decide to go along with me,
then, once I get what I want, I go away.
Or, if you decide not to work with me,

then I stay. Now, you know, I really like your mom. I like your house. It's a nice place. But I'm not sure how long I could put up with some of this stuff. Your sister seems fine, but I'm not a little-kid kind of guy." He sniffed and wiped at his nose. "Who knows? Maybe I'd grow to love it all. So if you don't go along with my plan, then I'll be making myself at home. My only problem with that is, I'd still have to figure out a way to make some cash."

"What plan?" I felt sick. The way War was talking sounded unlike anything he'd said before.

"I owe a bookie a few grand." He lit a cigarette, palm in front of his face to block the wind. "Eight thousand, to be exact."

"We don't have any money."

"You don't need money." He looked dead at me. "You're not really listening to me here. I need eight grand. And you're going to help me get it."

"Doing what?" I asked. Although by now I knew.

"We're going to run some tables, Shark. You're going to live up to your name." I didn't reply. "Or I stay." He pointed at the house. "I can figure out some other way to make money. You're just the fastest route. You decide. Meet me at the pool hall tomorrow at four, and we'll go with plan A. Or, I'll come back here and we'll see what plan B looks like." He clapped me on the shoulder and gave me a little shake. "Good talk, Shark. Good talk. We'll see you soon, one way or another." Then he got in his truck and drove away.

# Chapter Seven

I went to the pool hall the next day. I didn't have a choice. Once War had spelled it out for me, I knew that if I didn't do what he wanted, we'd never get rid of him. My mom couldn't take any more than she already had. Neither could Wendy. I had to be a man.

War smiled his great big grin when he came in and saw me dropping balls into the triangle. He put his hand on my shoulder.

"You made the right choice," he said. "Let's go."

"Where?"

"What, you thought you were going to shark people here? They already know how good you are." He lifted the triangle and scattered the balls. "Hippy, I'll cover whatever time he had."

"Sounds good," Hippy yelled. "Take it easy, Shark."

"Thanks, Hippy." We drove a couple of neighborhoods over, into a different world. The pool hall we stopped in front of looked like a slightly crappier Minnesota's. It was in an older building, and the stores on either side had been shut down and boarded up.

"Here's the plan," War said, shifting in his seat. "People like to throw down ten dollars here to start. You're just with me. You're my son, got it?" I hated that idea. I kept looking at him, hoping he'd quit all this. "Got it?"

"Whatever," I said.

"I'll do my best straight up against someone. Win or lose, it doesn't matter. You'll be on another table. Someone comes up, they'll ask me if they can play you. Whenever someone new comes in, you and I have a chat so everyone knows we're together. Then, if someone wants to play you, they'll ask me. I'll say, 'Sure, twenty-dollar minimum to play him.' You know, like it's a big joke. Then when they look at you, you say, 'I don't care' or whatever you want. Don't be cocky though. Then you get in there and you play your game and you fuck up all over the place. It's gotta be a serious mess. I'll start riding your ass about it. Calling you names. Telling you that you suck. I'll be that dad kids hate but maybe one day end up loving. Got me?" He knew what had happened with my dad. How intense he'd been with hockey. Neither my mom nor I had ever said anything about how dedicated Dad had been about helping me improve my skills. How calm he could be. To War, he was that crazy man in the stands who was always yelling.

"Fine," I said.

"Then the next game…" He eased up in his seat and pulled a twenty from his pocket. "I'm going to tell you that you're putting money on the next game so that maybe you'll think about actually trying. That it's your own cash and you have to spend it." He handed me the twenty, and I slid it into my pocket.

"Okay," I said.

"You're going to take that twenty and put it on the table, and then you're going to kick the guy's ass."

"What's twenty bucks?" I said.

"You don't have to destroy him. Bump it up a little. Leave some space so he thinks he has a chance. Then you leave the forty on the table. That's your next bet, and he'll have to match it if he wants to play again, and he will. That time you'll lose. And I'm going to lose my shit on you. At which time I'll slap a hundred down. And when he takes that bet, you are going to kick his ass."

"What's a hundred bucks when you need eight thousand?"

"It's a beginning. But it's also practice. You need to know how these things work. People get heated. You have to figure out where your emotions will go."

"Fine," I said, although it was anything but.

I didn't like it any more once we were inside. The same stale spilled-beer stink rose up around us. The crisp, tinny laughter. People chortling at inappropriate jokes.

I messed around on a table while War played, until finally a thick, crisp-looking dude came up, leaned into War and asked him something.

"Sure, go ahead, play him," War said, voice overly loud. "Don't need my permission." I played as crappily as possible. The guy introduced himself as Jimmy, and Jimmy was impossibly bad. It took more skill than ever to let him win. When the eight ball dropped, War was quick to light into me.

"Jesus Christ, son, what are you doing?" he yelled.

"What?" I replied, then stood still, looking frightened. His tone and the loudness and the anger in his voice all reminded me of my father in the worst way.

"What the hell was that?" War demanded.

"He played a pretty good game," Jimmy said. "He just got trapped around the corner."

"Trapped?" War said, staring daggers at me. "You couldn't figure out a way to get un-trapped?"

"It was a hard game," I said. I didn't like any of this. It was the reason I never played for money. There were few ways it could end well.

War said, "You have any money, son?"

"Yeah," I said through gritted teeth.

"What do you have?"

"Twenty," I said.

"You're playing him for twenty," War said.

"Nah, man, he's a kid," Jimmy said.

"He's a kid who has to get better," War said. "And he needs to have something on the line or that'll never happen. Twenty to play him."

"You okay with this, kid?" Jimmy asked. He had warm, round eyes. He looked like he wanted to give me a way out but didn't know how that'd look. I pulled the twenty from my pocket and put it on the table. "Keep that in your pocket, kid," he said. "They don't like us playing for money here." I slid the twenty back into my pocket. He flashed a twenty from his shirt pocket. It was all pretty awkward, but some guys like this stuff. I guess it feels as if they're breaking the law or something. As if they're putting it over on all the regular chumps of the world. "You want to break?"

"Sure," I said.

"Okay. You break." He began chalking his cue like crazy. I broke and played it slow. I ended up with a high ball in and potted three more before I skimmed the fourth. I didn't want it to look like a runaway. The table was perfect for me though. I could have sunk everything without breaking a sweat. But I didn't. Mostly because I was afraid of War.

Jimmy managed to get five balls in before he stalled. I sank another three before shanking again. He then put in one, evening things up. The eleven and the eight were perfectly set up. I fluffed on the eleven, managing to just get it in but looking totally inept. Then I hammered in the eight like an absolute amateur.

"There you go," Jimmy said. He came over and secretly pressed a twenty into my hand. "That was a better game."

I slid the twenty into my pocket.

"I could have had you," he said.

"It was tight," I said.

"Double down?"

"Yeah," I said. "Sure." It was playing out even better than War had expected.

This guy was pulling me in, not the other way around.

I threw the next game to the point where I had four balls left on the table when he was done. Jimmy was pretty pleased. War lost his shit. He took me into a corner and berated me. Made it look like he was clipping me on the back of the head. Then he stormed back over to Jimmy. And in his nicest, calmest voice he said, "I got a hundred bucks here says he'll win the next game."

Jimmy balked. "It doesn't seem fair."

"What do you care? The games have been tight. You don't want to take my money?"

"I don't think I want to be in the middle of this."

"The middle of what?" War said. "Everyone in here is betting on pool. You just bet on a game."

Jimmy looked at me. I was chalking one of the crappy pool-hall cues.

"Fine," Jimmy said. "One hundred. But I break."

"Go ahead," War said.

Jimmy broke and managed to drop three before screwing up. I ran the low balls, sinking the eight on a spinning shot that went off two walls before sending the white to gently settle in the middle of the table. Jimmy stood there staring at it. This is why I don't like sharking people. When it happens, they know. The question is, do they admit to it? The other problem with sharking someone is, you don't know how they're going to react.

I took the hundred from him. War was suddenly beside me. He looked at his watch. "Time we get out of here, son."

"Wait a second," Jimmy said. "You're not going to give me a chance to win it back?"

"We have to get going," War said, moving me toward and then out the door. We didn't get halfway to the truck before the door of the pool hall opened behind us and Jimmy came out.

"Hey, how come I ain't never seen either of you before?" That's when I noticed how War had parked the pickup. It was backed into a spot facing directly into the street. He'd been working every angle of this from the beginning.

War stepped up to Jimmy, grabbed his collar and said, "Don't be a sore loser." He shoved him backward. Jimmy opened his mouth, then shut it. War is a big dude. Big enough that you wouldn't want to mess with him alone. I felt bad for Jimmy. What War was here was a straight-up bully.

"Don't bring that shit around here again," Jimmy said. "It's bullshit." Then he went back into the pool hall.

"Give me the money," War said. He snatched the bills out of my hand. "I made twenty, so we cleared one hundred."

"One hundred," I said. "You said you needed eight thousand."

"I do," he said. He was angry, or at least riled up, from the recent encounter. "And we'll get it. This was a test. Let's get out of here before that guy finds some friends." We got in the truck. It started on the first turn, and in a second we were out of the lot and onto the street. "Tell your mom you're staying at a friend's place this weekend. We're going all around this city and making some serious money." He stepped on the gas, inhaled and then slowly, carefully, pulled into traffic.

## Chapter Eight

In the morning Mom let me know she had the weekend off. This didn't happen very often. For once she was going to be able to stay home, which worked perfectly for War's plan. I didn't even have to worry about leaving Wendy alone. I'd spent most of the night trying to figure a way out of this but knew there weren't any. So I made up an imaginary friend to go out with and lied to my mother.

"I might end up staying at his place," I said.

"How come I haven't met this friend before?" Mom asked.

"We ended up in a group at school. I've started hanging out with him. We have a project we need to get done." It all felt so awful. I hate lying to my mother. It was something my father did as well, always glancing at me to go along with him as he did it.

"Well, Wendy and I can have some girl time then." I wasn't certain how happy Wendy was with this idea. She hates doing her nails and stuff, but she will if Mom asks.

"Sounds great," I said.

Then, out of nowhere, Mom said, "Warren seems so nice. Doesn't he seem nice to you?"

"He's quite a guy," I admitted.

"You know I worry about you going into those pool halls. The kinds of people in some of them. But I think you found one of the good ones there."

"I guess so," I said. Mom left for work. I turned to my sister, who had been staring at me the whole time Mom had been talking.

"You really think Warren is that great?" she asked.

"I don't know," I said.

"There's something creepy about him. Isn't there?"

"Yeah," I admitted. She could read people. And I couldn't lie to her. "Don't worry—he won't be around much longer."

"I hope not. He gives me the shivers."

That afternoon War was waiting for me a block from my house. Wendy and I were coming down the street, and she was telling me all about the short story she was working on. I was listening so intently that I didn't even notice War until he stepped out of the pickup.

"Hey, Shark, let's get going," he said. Wendy stared at him.

"I thought you were going to a friend's place," she whispered.

"I am, Wendy. In a little bit. Warren and I have to do something first." The look on her face made me feel as if I'd let her down. But what could I do? I was entirely trapped. I made sure she had her house key, then watched her walk the rest of the way to our house and go inside.

"Okay," I said. "Let's get this over with."

"Cheer up, Sharky, it'll be fun!"

It wouldn't be fun.

The first place we hit was a giant pool emporium downtown. Forty tables spread out over a vast, organized space. Half of the tables were occupied at four thirty on a Friday. There were enough dudes standing around that it was obvious some betting was going on. All these men waiting for someone to challenge them. The majority of the TVs had sports on but also horse racing and off-track betting scores. It didn't take War long to find a ten-dollar game he could join. Here the bills sat on the table, and people leaned back and waited for someone to show and play. If you won, you owned the table and got to choose how much it cost to play. There was a free table beside the one War jumped on. I racked a set and started knocking balls around, waiting for someone to take up the challenge.

It wasn't long before we had the opportunity to run the game again. The dad, the kid. The only difference was that War told me to hold back. I could win, but it had to be tight. We wanted to extend the time I could play before people clued in to the fact that there was a kid at the hall sharking people.

We managed to run the act for almost three hours, pulling in a little over five hundred dollars. That was the thing with these big rooms—you could bounce around while people arrived and others left. You could tell that some of these guys had spent the whole day thinking about playing pool. Believing that tonight was the night they'd win big. Most of them didn't even seem to mind losing.

I took fifty dollars off a dude named Al who'd come off a shift at the nearby bakery and smelled of flour and vanilla. I was just jamming the money into my pocket when I noticed a couple of men looking at us strangely.

"We should get out of here, War," I said. "I think we're raising some suspicion."

"We're good," War said.

"Those guys have been watching us for a while. I don't think we should chance it." War looked at the two I'd indicated. I could tell he was checking them out for size and strength.

"You might be right," he said. He dug around in his pockets for his pack of cigarettes and lighter. He put a cigarette between his lips and brought the lighter up to it.

"No smoking in here," one of the bartenders said.

"Shit, yeah. The good old days are gone, aren't they, buddy?" he replied, slapping the bartender on the back. He pocketed his lighter and leaned in close to me. "Stick your phone to your ear and walk out of here. I'll be right behind you."

I did as he said, and no one bothered me. Soon enough War came out, and we got in his truck. It was parked the same way as the last time. Nose out, facing the exit. He planned for everything.

He had everything covered. I didn't ask what was next because I assumed it was going to be the same thing. Over and over, the same thing, until he had made his money. I would have to put up with it until he earned enough.

"First night and we're up eight hundred. Not bad for a start. A few of these places stay open late. I know a couple of backroom games as well, if we want."

"I don't think our little scheme will work in a backroom game," I said. My dad had taken me to a few of those before. He'd played clean. Never sharked anyone. He'd always played to the peak of his ability. And when he got sharked himself, he knew it. He'd point at whoever had sharked him and say, "Never again." And that was the end of it.

"The thing about backroom players, Shark," War said, reaching over and squeezing my shoulder, "is they're ready to be played. Everyone's a pro. It's not the amateur-hour stuff we're facing here." He suddenly turned down a side street. "And I think you're ready to give it a shot."

# Chapter Nine

We parked outside a deli and, to my surprise, went directly to the back entrance. War banged on the door and, just like in the movies, a little window opened.

"You back for more?" someone asked. War flicked his cigarette to the ground and jutted a thumb at me.

"The kid wants to play." All I could see through the slot were eyes.

"He good?"

"What do you care? Come on, let us in. It's freezing out here." The door opened, and we stepped inside. A tall, thin guy in black-framed glasses locked the door. We were on a landing at the top of a stairwell.

"What did you lose last time you were here?"

"I paid my bill."

The guy moved to the first step and looked back. "Word is, that's not always what happens."

War didn't respond, and eventually the thin guy shrugged his shoulders and moved down the stairs into the darkness.

"I'm not playing here," War whispered to me. "Just you. This isn't sharking. These dudes are the best you have ever played against. It's five hundred a game, so don't fuck up." He poked me in the chest, then went down the stairs.

Jeff Ross

The basement was well decked out. Dart boards, a long bar down one wall, a stereo playing old soul music off in a corner and a single snooker table in the center of the room. I quickly counted ten men. Two guys were playing a game, one was behind the bar in a tight tuxedo, and the rest stood around watching. When we stepped into the room, it seemed as if everyone stopped what they were doing to look at us.

"You're not welcome here," a big man in a suit and tie said to War.

"I'm not playing," War said. He put his hands on my shoulders and moved me forward. "He is."

The man looked at me. He held his pool cue in one hand and a triangle in the other. "Five hundred a game," he said. I felt my heart speed up.

"I didn't think it'd be any different," War replied.

"Where's his cue?"

I'd always wanted my own cue. But the problem was that if I got one, it would be something someone could take from me.

"I'll use whatever," I said, my voice catching and squeaking like a thirteen-year-old's. There was a gurgle of laughter.

"Can you loan him one, John?" War asked.

John stepped forward and handed me his cue. "This work for you?"

I took the cue, barely looking at it. "Sure."

Everyone laughed again. I had no idea what was so funny. "You can school us with any old cue, is that it?" John said. I guess I must have looked arrogant. But, honestly, the cue doesn't matter to me. A good one you're used to is always going to be better. But any cue that is basically straight will do.

"It looks like a nice cue," I said, studying it carefully for John's sake. I don't really get nervous when it comes to pool. I get excited, sometimes a little sweaty, but not, strictly speaking, nervous.

That night I was nervous.

John said, "Let's have a drink first. Though nothing with alcohol. I don't want to get in trouble with your mom." Everyone laughed again.

You'd think that with all the laughter, the place would feel pretty lively. That could not have been further from the truth. It felt to me at the time like a playground where a bully had squared off with some little kid and everyone with any sense was choosing the bigger guy's side in case things got ugly.

"We're on a bit of a schedule here," War said, looking at his oversized gold watch. "A ginger ale for the kid," he said to the bartender. "Rum for his manager."

War inhaled and exhaled as he crossed the room. "Throw some coke in it, would you?" he said as he pulled out a barstool. I sat down beside him and drew the ginger ale toward me.

"So War is managing you?" John asked. His breath smelled of whiskey. When I didn't answer right away, he gestured at the top shelf above the bar, where the bottles were clean and bright and almost entirely full. "Another, Pete." He accepted the glass and leaned against the bar. "Because I would suggest that's a horrible idea."

"Not your business, John," War said.

"This guy," John said without glancing at War, "is a man with a lot of plans and very little follow-through."

The music playing was a crazy, repetitive techno thing. There were three or four voices that kept singing the same lines over and over again, wrapping around one another until you couldn't tell what was being said. Honestly, it was beginning to play with my head a bit.

John leaned back hard on the bar and looked around the room. He took another pull from his drink, then said, "Who wants a shot at War's wonder boy?" No one immediately volunteered. "No one?" The song had changed to the Band's "The Weight," immediately making the room feel more like every other pool hall on earth. "All right, wonder boy, I guess it's you and me." He flicked his head toward the bartender, who produced a quarter and set it on his thumbnail. "We flip to see who breaks. You call."

The bartender, a bright-blue-eyed man with a half grin stapled on his face, said, "Ready?"

"Sure."

He flipped the coin, and I said, "Tails" as it reached its peak height. The coin landed softly in Pete's palm, and he clapped his other hand over it, then looked at John.

"Well, what is it?" John asked.

Pete opened his hand and presented the quarter, tails side up.

"Eight-ball or nine-ball?" John asked.

"Nine," I replied without thinking. In nine-ball, all you have to do is sink the nine. It doesn't matter when as long as you hit whatever ball is next in line first. I'd been working on my nine-ball break after seeing a pro on YouTube sinking the nine off the break. When that happens, you win and have the shortest game imaginable. I'd discovered during practice that if you hit the racked balls just right and the nine doesn't drop, it will at the very least be set up in the perfect position to finish the match quickly.

Pete stepped to the stereo. He put on some classical music, then moved to the table and began setting the balls in a triangle.

"You listen to classical music, wonder boy?" John asked.

"Sure," I said. Classic rock was a staple in pool halls, but my mom often listened to classical music on the radio in the mornings. I didn't know the composers or who was playing, but I could name a few pieces.

"Whatever," John said, laughing. "Isn't that what all the kids say these days?"

Pete was finished racking the balls. I looked down at the tight cluster of nine balls as I chalked my borrowed cue. Pete had used an eight-ball triangle to set the balls, and they weren't that tight. There was space between the two and three.

"Do you not have a nine-ball triangle?" I asked. I'd finished chalking. Bits of blue dust floated around me.

"Not good enough for you?" John said, leaning over the table.

"It's not frozen," I said, pointing at the space between the two and three. I noticed War tensing up beside me. John looked more closely at the balls.

"Seems good to me."

"You break then," I said.

The room felt as if it inhaled on itself. John was staring dead at me and standing way too close, and a wave of whiskey breath floated over me.

He sniffed and said, "Pete, grab the nine triangle, would you?" He never took his eyes off me. Pete came up behind John, who reached out a hand without looking back. He passed me the triangle.

"Be my guest."

"I'm breaking?" I asked.

"You won the toss, didn't you?" I racked the balls in the triangle, keeping them perfectly set and tight. I lifted the triangle off, all under John's watchful eye. "Look good now?" he asked.

"Perfect," I said.

John took a step back and held an arm out toward the end of the table. I set the cue ball in the right spot, bent down low to the table and, after two quick practice strokes, hammered the cue ball. It clocked off the one, and in a matter of maybe three seconds, the two, four and six dropped.

And then the nine.

# Chapter Ten

It was like all the air in the room evaporated at once. My dad had done this a couple of times in the past. There was skill involved, of course, but also a healthy dose of luck. If you could learn how to sink the nine ball off the break and endlessly do it, pool wouldn't be much of a game. You needed to hit the one ball in just the right way, but something beyond pure skill was required to steer it into a pocket.

"Well," John finally said. I couldn't figure out what he was going to do next. I honestly had no idea until he opened his mouth and laughed. "Well, shit! That was a hell of a shot." He came to me and clapped me on the back. "Was that shit luck, or did I just get sharked?"

"No sharking here," War said, coming off his barstool fast enough to topple it.

John held a hand up, and the room froze. "Well?"

"There was some luck involved," I said.

John leaned his cue against a chair and started gathering the balls. "Think you can get lucky twice?" he said.

"Another five," War said.

John tightened the balls in the triangle. "This isn't a practice hall,

Warren," he said. "Of course it will be another five."

"Just checking." War waited for a second and then said, "How about that first five?" I could hear John inhale from across the table. He removed the triangle, set it on its hook, then came around the table to me. He straightened to his full height and pulled a billfold from a pocket. It looked to be full of hundreds. He peeled off five and held them before me.

"Now you have something to play with," he said. "Because if history has taught me anything, your friend came in assuming you'd win that first game." He pressed the bills into my hand.

"I'll hold that," War said.

"We don't deal with managers here," John said, still not looking at War. "We flip for every game. No one owns the table. You okay with that?"

"Sure," I said.

"Go ahead, Pete," John says. "This time I call."

Pete flipped the coin. "Tails," John yelled.

"Tails it is," Pete said, maybe even before it landed in his palm. I moved aside to let John break. He hammered the cue ball, sending the other nine balls into a flurry of activity.

John moved like a cat around the table. It was weird to see a man of his size creeping around the table as though sneaking up on something. The break was fairly clean, by which I mean the balls arranged themselves in an agreeable way. There were plenty of shots available. The only real issue was the four ball, which was tight to the eight, halfway up one wall. John chalked his cue and roamed the outside of the table.

He dropped the one quickly and then the two. The three had gone down on the break, leaving him on the four.

"That one's a bit of a problem," John said, not looking at anyone. "A real dilemma." He glanced over at me before bending down to the side of the table. After practicing the shot a couple of times, he looked up at me and lightly tapped the cue ball. It rolled across the table and clinked off the four ball before rolling back slightly. I knew what he was going to do before he did it. He was snookering me. Or, at the very least, trying to set me up to be the one who banged the four off the wall and, very likely, failed to sink it. It was an impossible shot with the four so close to the eight. There was a chance I could get the eight and the four to drop, but the odds were low. They were too tight to one another and slightly offset.

But then I saw the angle. The nine was down the other end of the table, right on the edge of the pocket. So I had to hit the four, but if I put some major backspin on the cue ball, it could potentially roll straight back down the table and tap the nine in. The worst-case scenario would be that John ended up in about the same position I was in.

So basically I had nothing to lose.

The room had grown quiet. I leaned down at the side of the table and aimed right near the bottom of the cue ball. I knew it was going to work as soon as I hit the cue ball. It smacked into the four and came back like a pinball coming off a bumper. I stood quickly, bringing the cue up and out of the way. The cue ball rolled the length of the table and had just enough force left to tap in the nine.

John looked at me and then spit on the floor.

"Well, shit," he said. "Son of a bitch." He rubbed the back of his head and then threw his cue down.

"Get out of here, both of you," he said, pulling his money clip from his pocket. Bills scattered all over the place. He gathered them up, jammed five into my hand and shoved me toward the door.

# Chapter Eleven

"It's not that you're not welcome, War," John said to us out behind the deli. "It's just that no one wants you here." He gave War a shove. There were five men behind him, and I could tell War had little interest in turning this into an event he'd absolutely come out on the losing side of.

"But you can come back whenever you want, wonder boy," John continued.

"I'd like to see some of that magic again. Next time I'll get you to play someone else."

"Okay," I replied. John and the other men stepped back inside. The door shut with a slam. Something heavy and metal dropped on the other side.

"Give me the money," War said.

"Let's wait until we're in the truck," I replied.

"Give me the money now," War said, grabbing at my jacket pocket. I backed up and pulled the bills out of my jeans pocket. He snatched them out of my hand. "Get in the truck."

The headlights illuminated an empty street. It was getting late, and I was already tired. I didn't know how long I'd be able to play well. If the two games against John had taken much longer, I would have started having issues.

"That was a good bump," War said. "A quick grand. Let's hit this next place, then see if we can find another back-room game for when the halls close."

"I'm getting tired," I said.

"You'll be fine," War replied. "Get you a coffee or one of those stupid energy drinks kids love."

I didn't want coffee or an energy drink. But I also didn't want to talk to War, so I just sat there, quietly trying to wake myself up.

We drove through town to a different hall. This one was packed. Not a free table in sight. You had to win your way onto a table. War leaned on me as we stepped between two tables. On one a fifty-dollar bill sat beside the corner pocket, and on the other, a ten-dollar bill.

"We walk up to the tables and you go to the one with the fifty. I'll go to the ten. Then when we spot the bills, we'll pretend we made a mistake. And laugh

it off. These guys are going to eat it up."
I did as he said. The two at my table
were looking to play doubles.

"You even old enough to be in
here?" one of them asked.

"No one told me I couldn't be," I said.

"Name's Ron," the guy said. He
was short, shorter than me, but had a
fantastic beard and bright brown eyes.

"You old enough to play a fifty-
dollar game?" Ron's friend asked.

"Shit," War said. "I went to the
wrong table."

"Hey," the second guy said. "You
can swap."

"No," War said. "Fair's fair. Go
ahead, son." He gave me a wink to let
me know I could win if I wanted. It was
actually a challenge. Ron was really
good. Tight. But I still had an edge
on him. The hardest part of it all was
snookering him when he went for the
eight ball and I still had one on the table.

For once I had to figure out a strategy to not win, exactly, but make him lose. When it was done, I sat there with a hundred dollars in my pocket.

"Not bad," Ron said. "You play nine-ball?"

I was tired, and, as I'd yet again proved to myself, nine-ball takes way less time than eight.

Especially if you can sink the nine on the break.

"Sure," I said.

He racked up a game of nine-ball.

"I don't enjoy losing," Ron said in a kind of singsongy voice. He smelled of Old Spice, even in the stink of the hall. He was chewing a giant wad of gum. His buddy had a wad of chewing tobacco in his lip.

"Not many people do," I said.

Ron pulled out a crisp hundred-dollar bill and put it on the table. "Double or nothing," he said.

I looked at it. Hundred on the table. Hundred in my pocket.

Ron noticed my hesitation. "What? You were willing to lose fifty—may as well be willing to lose one hundred."

This was the kind of mentality that made me never want to gamble. It wasn't even close to logical. If you'd lost it once, you could lose it again. I glanced at War, who was pretending to be completely into the ten-dollar game.

"Okay," I said. "I guess."

"You guess?" Ron said. He looked at his buddy. "You think we're getting sharked here?" His buddy laughed and spit a wad of tobacco into an empty bottle.

"You never know, Ron."

"Winner breaks," Ron said, looking back at me.

After the break, it looked easy enough. Everything could be lined up. I mapped out the table. Where to move.

How to bring the cue ball back each time. The only difficulty was going to be the seven, which was sitting in the middle of the table. But I figured it should be easy enough to crack it into a corner eventually. I took my time between shots, chalking my cue as I went. In the end, it was as easy as I thought it was going to be. The seven was a bit of a challenge, but once it dropped, the eight and nine were set up perfectly. I cleared the table and took a seat.

"Yup," Ron said. "That's how you play nine-ball." I could tell he was trying to decide if he should play again. He watched me put the two hundred in my pocket.

"The balls were lined up nicely," I said.

"I guess they were." He leaned his cue against the table. "Let's do it again. Five hundred this time."

War jumped in. "Whoa! What's this?"

"He has two hundred in his pocket," Ron said. He suddenly looked mean. "I want to put five hundred on the next game."

"What's the game?" War asked.

"Nine-ball."

War leaned back against his table. Sniffed. "What do you think, son?"

I hated the way he called me son. It filled me with a rage I had to fight to control.

"Whatever," I said.

"How was the last game?"

"He cleared the table. I didn't get a chance to play," Ron said.

War kept watching me. "You ran the table?"

I nodded. Ron stared at War, never looking at me.

"It'll be my money, not his," War said, and Ron shrugged. "His game, his break."

Ron popped in a new piece of gum. Stared at me. Then looked back at War. "I can abide by that," he said.

"Let's do it then," War said.

I almost wanted to fail at this game just to make War angry. Just to have him lose. He looked so confident. But he was like a sports fan cheering on his team, yelling at the opposition's fans as if he'd actually done something other than just watch a game. He could be confident in my winning, but in the end the win was mine—even if he got to take the money.

I broke and made it as far as the four before running into a problem. The five was up behind the eight, and although I bounced the cue ball off two walls, the five came up short. Luckily, the cue landed behind the six, meaning it would be almost impossible to get the five. Ron spent a long time rubbing his beard and then setting up his shot before sending the cue ball careening up the table. I watched as it came back, clacked into the five and set it into a corner pocket.

"Ho, shit, this dude can play," he said, as if he were a spectator watching himself play. It's always weird to me when people refer to themselves in the third person. It seemed to pump him up, though, because soon enough he was strutting around like Tom Cruise in The Color of Money. The six and seven were set up tight to one another. Ron spent a long time trying to figure out how to play it, his beard getting another complete work-over. A crowd had formed, drawn in by the bills on the table. This was the last thing War and I wanted. You need to keep away from these high-profile games. You want to be mentioned but not well known. Ron managed to hit the six, but it bounced off the edge of the hole and just sat there, waiting for an easy tap in.

"Fucker," he said, banging his cue against the floor.

I got the six and the seven with ease. The eight was in a bad spot though. But the angles started to form on the table for me like vibrant glowing lines. I knew I could do it. I sent the cue ball down and tapped the eight perfectly into a corner pocket. It was an impressive shot, one my dad had taught me years before. In pool there are shots you can make if you know how to hit the cue ball, how to give it some spin. And then there are shots you'll never get until you've tried them a thousand times. This was one of those shots. It was the kind of shot someone could only make if they'd devoted far too much of their life to this game.

The nine was right beside a corner pocket. I took my time, chalking my cue and snapping my neck. My cue didn't really need chalk and my neck was fine, but I wanted to draw this out a little. I wanted to make War wait. I guess, in the end, I needed a little drama. Something to make it feel like I'd defeated some great competitor. I lined the shot up, tapped the cue ball and dropped the nine lightly into a pocket.

"What the fuck?" Ron said. "I've never seen a shot like that in my life." He looked really angry. He was, of course, talking about the eight ball, not the nine. But he was decent enough to hold back his anger until I'd calmly sunk the nine.

"Calm down, buddy," War said.

"This is bullshit."

"He hasn't lost a game yet," War said. "What made you think he was suddenly going to suck?"

"He was good in the other games, maybe even great," Ron said. "But that shot on the eight? That was beyond impossible."

"Listen, buddy—" War said.

"Don't call me buddy."

War held his hands up. The atmosphere in the room had changed. It'd turned ugly. These guys were obviously regulars. A couple of real hotshots. "What is he, some kind of junior champ?" Ron demanded.

"Listen," War said. "What do you think is happening here?"

"I think I'm getting sharked."

"To me it looks more like you've just lost." We were up quite a bit. But that was the problem with sharking. We were up, which meant someone else had to be down.

Ron turned to his friend. "You saw him?"

"Yeah," his friend said.

"Buddy," War said. "He never lost. To be sharked you need to be reeled in. Your opponent has to lose a couple of games, make you think you're top shit.

That's not what happened here. All that's happened is that you lost, thought you could beat him, didn't, still believed in yourself and lost again." I could see War eyeing the door, considering his escape. He didn't want to be there much longer. This place was burned. We were up over two grand. Another three or four places and we'd make the eight he needed, and War would be out of my life. That was all I could think while standing there staring at the green felt of the pool table. Another few wins, and War would be out of my life.

"Listen, let's forget about it," I said. "Let's go."

"Now you're going to leave?" Ron said.

"You want another game?" War replied. "Five hundred dollars. That's what you set."

Ron looked at me. Pointed his finger in my face. "Fuck you," he said.

He turned to War. "Fuck you too. Come in here sharking people."

"He. Hasn't. Lost," War said. He sounded insulted. As if we hadn't come into the pool hall looking to shark people. As if, somehow, we'd actually been wronged. "If anyone is being sharked, it's us."

I didn't want any part of it. I mean, I knew I could take this guy. But I didn't like all the aggression around it.

"I'm not playing him again," I said to War. "Forget it."

"There you go," War said. "It's over. Let's go, son." We dropped our cues on the table and walked to the door. People parted to let us through. We made it all the way up the stairs to the door. I opened the door, and a rush of noise from a truck on the street swept in, which I guess is why we didn't hear Ron coming up the stairs behind us. When the truck had passed, the next sound

I heard was a cue hitting the back of War's head. Someone tried to grab me. I shrugged him off and darted out the door. Someone yelled at me. I bounced side to side, trying to figure out what to do. But then I just started running.

I must have gone three blocks before I spotted a bus slowing for a stop. When the doors opened I hopped on, flashing my pass as I ran past the driver and into a seat. I pulled my hoodie over my head and then sat there trying to get my breathing under control. Trying to figure out what had happened and what the hell I was going to do next.

# Chapter Twelve

War wasn't at my house the next day, and I immediately began to wonder what had happened to him. I wasn't worried. Whatever happened to him he had coming. Either he'd weaseled his way out of a confrontation or had his ass handed to him. In the end, I didn't feel it had anything to do with me.

I had a great day hanging out with my mom and sister. We watched a movie together that night, all curled up on the couch, something we hadn't done in years. It wasn't until Sunday morning, right around the time I started thinking War was gone for good, that there was a hammering on the door. I looked out my window and saw War's pickup out in the street. Wendy was awake, standing in my room.

I gave her my cell phone. "Anything happens, you call the police, okay?" I said. "Stay in here. Hide in the closet if you have to." I hated doing this to her. Filling her with fear again.

"Who is that hammering?" Mom called.

"Mom, leave it," I yelled as I ran out of the room. But I was too late. She'd already opened the door. War busted into the room, looking like hell. He had a black eye, a bruised cheek, a long cut across his forehead. His left arm was in a cast. He was scruffy again, hunkered in his leather jacket.

"You little fucker," he said. "You screwed that up."

"Warren!" Mom said.

"You shut up," War snarled.

"Don't talk to my mom like that."

Mom seemed to want to speak but just stood there, looking stunned.

"Oh, now you're going to stand up to me?"

I could see something in his eyes. The same thing I'd seen in the eyes of the hockey dad just before he'd swung at my dad that day. Pure rage. This was directed right at me. It felt awful. It felt as if I was falling back in time, and all the feelings and emotions were rolling back out. Ready to swallow me.

War was big. But I made a quick assessment and decided that if it came to it, especially with the one arm in a sling, he wouldn't destroy me.

He came at me and grabbed my collar.

"Warren!" Mom yelled.

War spun me around, hitting a lamp and sending it smashing to the floor.

"You abandoned me, you little shit." I didn't reply. I didn't have anything to say. "We're doubling the amount I need now. Sixteen."

He had me in a one-armed bear hug. I brought my arms up and smashed them back into his stomach. He let go immediately. I spun around to face him. He was holding his injured arm, his face still twisted with that rage.

"We're over," I said. "I have nothing to do with this."

"Yes you do, son. I'm in your life now."

"Warren," Mom pleaded. "Mark, what's going on?"

"I'm not doing it again," I said. "That's not how I play."

"You will, or I'll make your lives a living hell."

He came at me again, his arm raised. He could hit me, that I knew. But I didn't care. I wasn't giving in to him. I wasn't giving in to a bully. I was not going to be the victim of someone else's anger.

I brought my leg up as he approached and drove my foot into his knee. He fell sideways, taking a side table with him. He swung as he went down and caught me on the side. I fell back, smashing into the mirror that covered the hall closet door. A second later he was up again, hobbling toward me. He was about to throw another punch, one that would certainly have knocked me out, but my mother grabbed his arm. He shrugged her off, and when she came at him again he tossed her to the side, sending her headfirst into a wall. I was so angry that I jumped up and ran dead into him. But he was bigger and stronger, and a moment later I was pinned beneath him again. He had his fist raised, ready to drive it into my face, when I heard the sirens.

One of the things that had appealed to my mom about the little house she'd found when she decided to move us here was that it was only a block away from a police station. Not one of those little community ones either, but a real one. One where officers were always coming and going. Where someone was always around. So when Wendy called the police, officers were dispatched from less than a block away.

War was dragged away in cuffs. Mom and I each told our story of what had happened. I had to sit there in front of her and tell her about the gambling. About how War had promised he'd be a never-ending part of our lives if I didn't play along. She looked as if she was about to cry. The giant bump on her forehead was awful to see. Maybe the worst thing ever.

I had a broken rib and various cuts on my face and arms, which was no fun for me but much worse for War. I'm seventeen, which meant he'd come into our home and assaulted a minor.

When the police were done with their questions and everyone had left, my mom said, "I had no idea." It was just the three of us again, the family.

"I'm sorry," I said.

"It's not your fault," she said. "He should never have preyed on a kid."

I didn't know what else to say. The police told us that that War was going to be in jail for quite some time, probably somewhere upstate. Assault on a minor is pretty serious, especially when you are already on probation. Since he wasn't from around here originally, the police said it was unlikely we would ever hear from him again.

That's what we would hope for. That War would disappear from our lives completely.

# Chapter Thirteen

When Hippy asked, I told him the whole story. At first I wasn't going to. I mean, it's embarrassing, right? The way War inserted himself into our lives. The way he took advantage of me.

The way he made me do things I swore I would never do.

Hippy laid a hand on my shoulder and shook his head.

"And here you are," he said. "Right?"

"Right." I leaned down to take my shot and thought about those words. *And here you are.* That was the point, right? It was shit. I'd made some poor choices, but here I was.

It all could have been worse in countless ways.

Mom has decided to visit Dad in prison. They've talked on the phone a few times in the past few weeks, but she has yet to actually go visit. It isn't that she blames him for what happened. It was an accident, after all. But it was an accident that could have been avoided. He could have managed his anger. He could have left it all alone.

He could have let me stand up for myself that day rather than getting in the middle of it all.

"I should have told my mom what was happening," I said to Hippy.

"You did what you did, man. It's behind you now. Yeah, learn from it,

I guess. But don't beat yourself up about it."

"Okay, whatever you say." I banged the four and then the eight into a side pocket and straightened.

"I'm going to beat you one of these days," Hippy said.

"Whatever you say," I replied, laughing.

We have not seen War again. Apparently, he was released on bail and then disappeared. The officer who came to our house the night of the fight returned to fill us in. Turned out old War was wanted in a couple of other states too. He'd likely gone someplace where the police didn't know about him.

You won't see him around here, the officer said. But if you do, give us a call. And that was that.

I can tell Mom wishes Dad was around. We didn't tell him anything about the whole mess. He is in counseling, working on his anger, and we were worried that if he heard about it, his guilt at being unable to protect us would push him over the edge again.

None of this has helped Wendy at all. She is still afraid of men and likely will be for a long time to come. She has dug into her art and hides in her room after school, reading books. And she has never talked to me about anything that happened that night. I think she will someday, but in her own time.

As for me, I'm fine. I wish I could say I'm great. But I feel awful about how I behaved. I could have reached out for help. I could have talked to Mom or Hippy or even the police. I didn't have to do all of that alone. I didn't have to let myself be sucked in. I didn't have to do what someone told me to do because he said he owned me.

No one owns me. I will never allow someone to think that again. If I learned anything at all from this, it's that you can't let people push you around.

But, at the same time, you don't have to push back either.

Jeff Ross is an award-winning author of several novels for young adults, including the Orca Soundings titles *Coming Clean* and *A Dark Truth*. He currently teaches scriptwriting and English at Algonquin College in Ottawa, Ontario, where he lives with his wife and two sons. For more information, visit www.jeffrossbooks.com.

Titles in the Series

# orca soundings